AUDREY WOOD **THE NAPPING**

Illustrated by
DON WOOD **HOUSE**

HARCOURT BRACE JOVANOVICH, PUBLISHERS

San Diego   New York   London

Library of Congress Cataloging in Publication Data
Wood, Audrey.
    The napping house.
    Summary: In this cumulative tale, a wakeful flea atop a number
of sleeping creatures causes a commotion, with just one bite.
    [1. Sleep — Fiction. 2. Fleas — Fiction] I. Wood, Don,
1945 —   ill. II. Title.
PZ7.W846Na   1984   [E]   83-13035
ISBN 0-15-256708-9

Printed in the United States of America

First edition

A   B   C   D   E

The book was printed by offset on 80 lb. Karma Text.
The original paintings were done in oil on pressed board.
The text is Clearface Roman, set by Thompson Type,
    San Diego, California.
The display type is Clearface Bold, set by Thompson Type,
    San Diego, California.
Separations were made by Heinz Weber, Inc., Los Angeles,
    California.
Printed by Holyoke Lithograph, Springfield, Massachusetts.
Bound by Book Press.
Designed by Dalia Hartman.

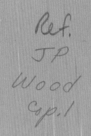

For Maegerine Thompson Brewer

There is a house,
a napping house,
where everyone is sleeping.

And in that house
there is a bed,
a cozy bed
in a napping house,
where everyone is sleeping.

And on that bed
there is a granny,
a snoring granny
on a cozy bed
in a napping house,
where everyone is sleeping.